Get Around

in Air and Space

Get Around
in Air and Space

by Lee Sullivan Hill

Carolrhoda Books, Inc./Minneapolis

For my son Adam, for his invaluable assistance.
—L. S. H.

For more information about the photographs in this book, see the Photo Index on pages 30–32.

The photographs in this book are reproduced through the courtesy of: © Cheryl Walsh Bellville, cover, pp. 2, 13, 18, 26, 27, 28, 29; © William B. Folsom, pp. 1, 6, 8, 9, 15, 19; © Roger J. Ritchie/Flight Safety International, Inc., p. 5; © Carl Schuppel/ Experimental Aircraft Association, p. 7; Visuals Unlimited: (© McCutcheon) p. 10, (© John Sohlden) p. 14, (© Charles Newman) p. 16; © John Splettstoesser, p. 11; © Buddy Mays/Travel Stock, p. 12; © Wisconsin Department of Natural Resources, p. 17; © NASA, pp. 20, 21, 22, 23, 24, 25.

Text copyright © 2000 by Lee Sullivan Hill

Carolrhoda Books, Inc.
A Division of the Lerner Publishing Group
241 First Avenue North, Minneapolis, MN 55401 U.S.A.

Website address: www.lernerbooks.com

Library of Congress Cataloging-in-Publication Data

Hill, Lee Sullivan, 1958–
    Get around in air and space / by Lee Sullivan Hill.
        p.   cm. — (A get around book)
    Includes index.
    Summary: Explains why people travel in air and space and introduces the
various forms of transportation used.
    ISBN 1-57505-310-1
    1. Aeronautics, Commercial—Juvenile literature. 2. Space flight—Juvenile
literature. [1. Air travel. 2. Space flight.] I. Title. II. Series: Hill, Lee Sullivan,
1958–   Get around book.
HE9776.H55   2000   99-12542
629.13—dc21

Manufactured in the United States of America
1 2 3 4 5 6 - SP - 05 04 03 02 01 00

Transportation moves people and goods. By air, they get there quickly.

Some aircraft carry people. Big jets hold hundreds of passengers. They fly a thousand miles in just a few hours.

Light planes have room for three or four people. They fly more slowly than jets and travel shorter distances.

Commuter planes zip back and forth between cities. People can fly to work in another city and come back home at night.

Supersonic jets fly faster than the speed of sound. They whisk passengers from New York to Paris in less than four hours!

Some aircraft carry goods instead of people. Cargo planes are loaded with boxes and bags. Letters, fresh flowers, and fish travel quickly all over the world.

Cargo planes have open areas inside. They can hold big things such as horses and trucks. Some planes even carry other aircraft!

Sometimes air transportation comes to the rescue.
Coast Guard helicopters save people from sinking ships.

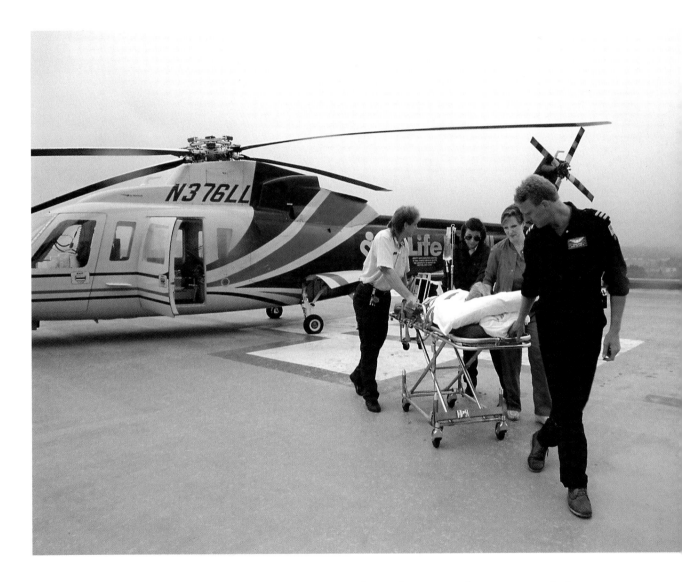

Some helicopters rescue people who are hurt or sick.
They can reach a faraway hospital quickly.

Aircraft help people work, too. Helicopters lift heavy
equipment to places that cranes can't reach.

Helicopters can carry cameras. Movie and TV crews take pictures from high in the sky.

Some aircraft have special jobs. Fire-fighting planes drop water or chemicals on raging forest fires.

Crop dusters spray farmers' fields. The spray kills weeds and helps crops grow.

Military aircraft fly for their countries. Small, speedy jets dart and dodge to keep out of trouble.

A stealth jet has another way to stay safe—it hides.
Its unusual shape makes a stealth jet hard for
enemies to find.

Some transportation flies into space. Rockets blast off with a burst of fire and steam. They lift a space shuttle up and away.

Space shuttles circle around Earth. Scientists study life on board the shuttle and on the planet below.

Space shuttles also deliver supplies to a space station.
Scientists live and work there for months at a time.

Sometimes astronauts must walk in space to make repairs. A special kind of rope keeps the astronaut from floating away.

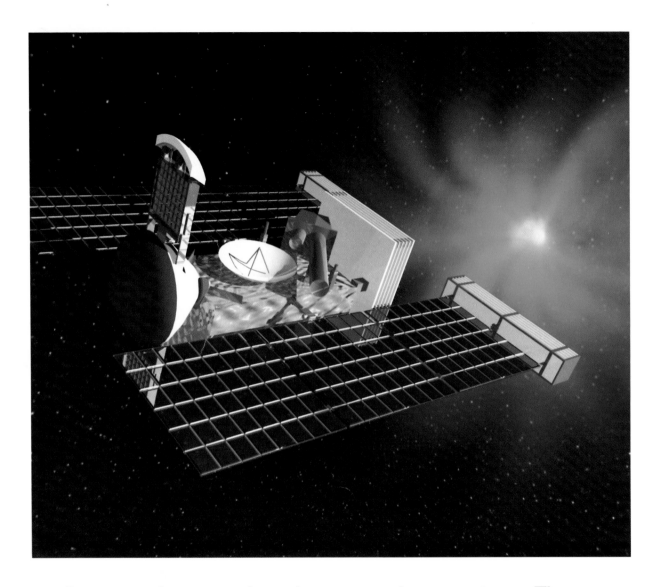

Space probes travel to places people cannot go. They send information back to scientists on Earth.

Space probes study planets, moons, and comets. They can even travel close to the Sun.

Sometimes getting around is just for fun. Hot air balloons float low in the sky. From a balloon, houses and cars look like toys.

Gliders sail silently in the clouds. They fly without an engine. Tow planes pull them up in the air and set them free to glide.

Transportation flies over mountains, seas, and into space beyond. Are you ready to fly?

Get around in air and space. See the world in a whole
new way.

Photo Index

Cover A helicopter can fly forward, backward, sideways, and straight up or down. This helicopter is used to spray chemicals on crops. Aircraft that spray crops are often called crop dusters.

Page 6 This Boeing 757 carries about 200 passengers. It can fly from Chicago to Boston (about 1,000 miles) in two and a half hours. The same trip would take 20 hours by car.

Page 1 This commuter plane is on a runway at Reykjavik Airport in Iceland. Commuter planes travel fairly short distances on a regular schedule. This one carries 16 passengers.

Page 7 Unlike most planes, this one runs on the same kind of gas that cars use. It is a home-built model that holds only one person. People can order the parts from a company called Foxbat and build the plane themselves.

Page 2 Hot air balloons are made of a light, silky fabric. A propane gas burner heats the air inside the balloon. The hot air rises and lifts the balloon and its basket of passengers.

Page 8 This Beechcraft 1900C is about to land at an airport in Portland, Maine. The three wheels of its tricycle landing gear have been lowered into position, and flaps on its wings have been raised to slow down the aircraft.

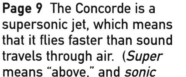

Page 5 The Piper Twin is a light plane that holds four passengers. It is also known as a twin-engine plane because it has two engines that power its pair of propellers.

Page 9 The Concorde is a supersonic jet, which means that it flies faster than sound travels through air. (*Super* means "above," and *sonic* means "sound.") The Concorde's small body was designed for speed, not comfort. Only 22 passengers can squeeze into the small cabin.

Page 10 Federal Express flies cargo all over the world. This B-727 jet is being loaded at Anchorage International Airport in Alaska. You can tell that it was built for cargo because it has no windows.

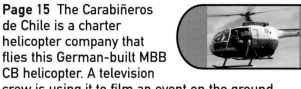
Page 15 The Carabiñeros de Chile is a charter helicopter company that flies this German-built MBB CB helicopter. A television crew is using it to film an event on the ground in Puerto Montt, Chile.

Page 11 This LC-130 cargo plane belongs to the United States Army. It has skis that allow it to land on snowy Mount Ellsworth in Utah. The crew is unloading a Huey UH-IN helicopter down the back ramp.

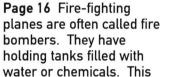
Page 16 Fire-fighting planes are often called fire bombers. They have holding tanks filled with water or chemicals. This one is dropping chemicals on a forest fire.

Page 12 The U.S. Coast Guard uses several kinds of helicopters for rescues. This photo shows a French-built Dolphin helicopter on a practice mission off the coast of Seattle, Washington.

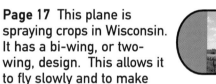
Page 17 This plane is spraying crops in Wisconsin. It has a bi-wing, or two-wing, design. This allows it to fly slowly and to make tight turns, which is useful for a crop duster.

Page 13 This medical transport helicopter just landed on the roof of the University of Minnesota Hospital in Minneapolis. The patient may have been moved from a smaller hospital or rescued from the scene of an accident.

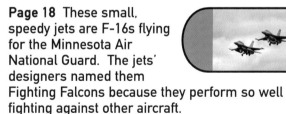
Page 18 These small, speedy jets are F-16s flying for the Minnesota Air National Guard. The jets' designers named them Fighting Falcons because they perform so well fighting against other aircraft.

Page 14 This Sikorsky Skycrane is lifting a ventilation unit to the top of a building in Topeka, Kansas. Before lifting, the pilot drains most of the helicopter's fuel. This makes it lighter, which allows it to lift up to 20,000 pounds of equipment.

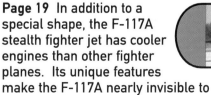
Page 19 In addition to a special shape, the F-117A stealth fighter jet has cooler engines than other fighter planes. Its unique features make the F-117A nearly invisible to enemy radar.

Page 20 This rocket blasted off from the Kennedy Space Center in Florida on October 18, 1993. Its purpose was to lift a space shuttle away from Earth's gravity and into orbit around Earth.

Page 21 Russian cosmonauts on the *Mir* space station took this photo of the space shuttle *Atlantis.* The cylinder inside the shuttle at the left is Spacelab, where astronauts perform scientific experiments.

Page 22 The space shuttle *Atlantis* is shown preparing to dock with the Russian space station *Mir* on July 4, 1995. *Atlantis* picked up American astronaut Norm Thagard, who returned home after living in space for several months.

Page 23 Astronauts walked in space to repair the Hubble Space Telescope on a mission in December 1993. An astronaut inside the space shuttle controls the movements of the space walker.

Page 24 This is an artist's drawing of the *Stardust* space probe. Scientists plan to have the probe collect dust from a comet's tail.

Page 25 An artist created this drawing of the SOHO space probe. It was launched in 1995 to study the Sun. SOHO orbits the Sun in a path between Earth and the Sun—about a million miles away from Earth.

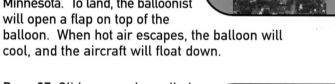

Page 26 This hot air balloon is floating over the Mississippi River town of Hastings, Minnesota. To land, the balloonist will open a flap on top of the balloon. When hot air escapes, the balloon will cool, and the aircraft will float down.

Page 27 Gliders are also called sailplanes. They have wide wings and small, light bodies that allow them to soar without engine power. The sailplane in this photo has a wingspan of about 50 feet.

Page 28 This Piper Cub is a classic J-3 model that was once used to train new pilots. Many World War II pilots learned to fly in Cubs. The first Cubs were built in 1928, but the J-3 model designed in 1938 became the most popular.

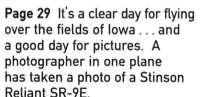

Page 29 It's a clear day for flying over the fields of Iowa . . . and a good day for pictures. A photographer in one plane has taken a photo of a Stinson Reliant SR-9E.